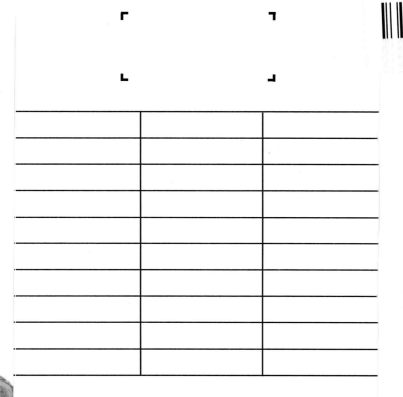

9 40467954

For my Michael with love xx
C.F.

For my Mum. I miss you every day! x
A.F.

A TEMPLAR BOOK

First published in the UK in 2018 by Templar Publishing,
an imprint of Kings Road Publishing, part of the Bonnier Publishing Group,
The Plaza, 535 King's Road, London, SW10 0SZ
www.bonnierpublishing.com

Text copyright © 2018 by Claire Freedman
Illustration copyright © 2018 by Alison Friend

1 3 5 7 9 10 8 6 4 2

ISBN 978-1-78370-645-7 (Hardback)
ISBN 978-1-78370-644-0 (Paperback)

This book was typeset in Adobe Caslon

Designed by Genevieve Webster
Edited by Alison Ritchie

Printed in China

BEAR'S STORY

CLAIRE FREEDMAN & ALISON FRIEND

templar
books

Once upon a time there was a bear
whose favourite thing to do was read.

But Bear had a problem; he had read his big book of stories
so many times, it was falling to pieces . . .

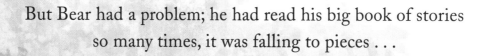

. . . and one day a sudden gust of wind blew all the pages away!

There was nothing else for it – Bear would have to make up his own story.
He fetched a pencil and a notebook then sat down to write.

The stories in his book all had exciting beginnings, dramatic middles
and happy-ever-after endings. But Bear didn't know where to begin.
The more he stared at the paper, the more it stared back at him.

Maybe all ideas start with a good back-scratch, he thought.
So he set off to find the perfect tree.

Bear was having a good old scratch when Mouse
came twirling along the blossomy path.

"Hello, Bear!" she called.
"I've got to practise my dancing for the Mouse Ball.
Can you help?"

So Bear got up on his tip-toes and he whirled and swirled
with Mouse until they were both out of breath.

"Thank you, Bear," said Mouse.
"No problem!" replied Bear.

But Bear did have a bit of a problem. Even though he had had
a good back-scratch, he could NOT think of a single idea for his story.

Maybe all ideas start with a nice dip in the river, he thought.

Bear was swimming about in the water when Rabbit appeared.

"Help me, Bear!" she called out. "I've dropped my oars!"

Bear grabbed the rope and pulled Rabbit's boat to shore.

"Thank you, Bear!" said Rabbit.
"No problem!" replied Bear.

But Bear did have a bit of a problem. Even though he had had a swim
AND a back-scratch, he still could NOT think of a single idea for his story.

Maybe all good ideas start with tree-climbing, he thought.

Bear set off to find the tallest tree in the forest,
and he began to climb.

He had nearly reached the top when . . .

"Toooo wit – tooo woo! Help!"
came a squeaky little voice.
Baby Owl was stuck on a branch and
couldn't get back to the nest.

Bear gently picked him up and put him safely back
with his brother and sister.

"Thank you, Bear!" squeaked Baby Owl.
"No problem!" replied Bear.
But Bear did have a bit of a problem because he STILL had absolutely
NO IDEAS for his story.

And now his tummy was rumbling.
Time for a snack, he thought and set off for home.

When he was nice and full, he sat down again to write.
The paper was still blank when some blossom
floated in through the open window.

That's when Bear suddenly remembered his adventures
with Mouse and Rabbit and Baby Owl.

Maybe all good ideas start with REAL adventures! he thought.
Bear began to scribble and scribble.

And he didn't stop scribbling until the sun went down and his story was finished.
Just then, there was a knock at the door.

Bear's new friends were standing on his doorstep with a big basket of berries.
"Thank you for helping us, Bear," they said.
"No!" said Bear. "Thank YOU for giving me ideas for my story!"

BEAR'S STORY
by Bear

Once upon a time a band of pirates set sail looking for treasure.
The captain was Redbeard Rabbit.
"Arrhh! Shiver me timbers and avast, me hearties!" she roared.

Mighty Mouse had the map.
"X marks the spot!" she cried,
dancing a little jig.

The One-Eyed Owls were
on look-out in the crow's nest.
"Land ahoy!" they called.

Barnacle Bear swam to the island, dug up the treasure chest
and pulled it back to the ship.

It was filled with goblets, coins and glittering jewels.
"Hoorah for the Swashbuckling Crew!" they cheered.

And they all lived happily ever after.

THE END

"A story! Ooooo! Toooo wit – tooo woo!
Read it to us! Please, Bear, please!"

So that's what Bear did.

"I like the beginning!" said Mouse.
"And the middle!" said Rabbit.
"And the happy-ever-after ending!" squeaked the baby owls.
They all agreed that it was a VERY GOOD story.
"Let's have more adventures," they said, "then Bear can write more stories!"

And that's exactly what they did.